COWBOY
NED & ANDY

DAVID EZRA STEIN

A PAULA WISEMAN BOOK
SIMON & SCHUSTER BOOKS FOR YOUNG READERS
NEW YORK LONDON TORONTO SYDNEY

SIMON & SCHUSTER BOOKS FOR YOUNG READERS
An imprint of Simon & Schuster Children's Publishing Division
1230 Avenue of the Americas, New York, New York 10020

Book design by Einav Aviram
The text for this book is set in Clearface.
The illustrations for this book are rendered in ink and watercolor.
Manufactured in China
2 4 6 8 10 9 7 5 3 1
Library of Congress Cataloging-in-Publication Data
Stein, David Ezra.
Cowboy Ned & Andy / David Ezra Stein.— 1st ed.
p. cm.
"A Paula Wiseman book."
Summary: On a cattle drive in the desert on the night before Cowboy Ned's birthday, his horse, Andy, goes in search of a birthday cake,
which he thinks will make Ned's birthday complete.
ISBN-13: 978-1-4169-0041-2
ISBN-10: 1-4169-0041-1
[1. West (U.S.)—Fiction. 2. Horses—Fiction. 3. Cowboys—Fiction. 4. Friendship—Fiction. 5. Deserts—Fiction.] I. Title.
PZ7.S8179Cow 2007
[E]—dc22
2005006969

To Pat and Paula, with deepest gratitude

Cowboy Ned and his trusty horse, Andy, were driving their cattle along the edge of the desert.

They rose before dawn and woke the cows.

The day grew hot.

They moved in a long train over the dusty earth.

At noon they drank from a cool river.

When night came, they were one day farther from home.

Cowboy Ned wrapped his poncho tight in the evening cool.

Andy munched his oats.

Ned stared at the faraway hills and sighed.

"Tomorrow is my birthday, Andy. I'll be another year older, and no one is around to celebrate. I miss my sister, Nedna; my brother, Nedrick; and my mother—we just call her Ma. Well, I'm glad you're here, Andy. Good night."

He quenched the campfire, and they lay down in the dark and quiet.

Andy tried to sleep but couldn't.

Something was bothering him.

"Tomorrow is Ned's birthday," he said to himself. "And the best thing to have on your birthday is a birthday cake. Ned needs a birthday cake, and I am going to find him one.

"And," he decided, "I'd better find one now, before he wakes up."

As quietly as he could canter, Andy slipped away from the campsite, and soon he was alone in the desert.

On the breeze he heard a shrill song.
It was a cricket, singing on a rock.

"Good evening," said Andy. "And would you have such a thing as a birthday cake about? I need one for my friend Cowboy Ned so he can have cake on his birthday."

"No," said the cricket in a wispy voice. "All I have in the world is my song." And he went on singing.

Andy walked on. It was cold and clear
and the moon was out.

Suddenly two big eyes shone from the darkness.

It was an owl, who sat on a cactus.

"I saw you coming a long way off," said the owl.
"What brings a young horse like you into
the desert at night?"

"I'm looking for a birthday cake for my friend Cowboy
Ned so he can have cake on his birthday," said Andy.

"I can see far and wide," said the owl, "from the
rising mountains to the rolling prairie, and I have
seen no birthday cake in this desert. Farewell."

And he closed his eyes.

Andy walked on. He was far from camp now, and it
seemed that dawn was close at hand.

"Oh, how I wish I had a birthday cake for my friend Cowboy
Ned so he could have cake on his birthday," said Andy.

Just then, a voice came from the dusty rock below.
"Who's that clattering around in the sky?" it hissed.

"It's me, Andy, the dapple gray steed," said Andy.

He looked down to find a scorpion at his feet, surrounded by stones.

"What do you want, clomping around here, you great four-legged clod?" asked the scorpion, not too politely.

"I'm searching for a birthday cake for my friend Cowboy Ned so he can have cake on his birthday," said Andy.

"I have no birthday cake around here," snipped the scorpion. "I have only my stones, stones and dust, and I'd thank you to go away and let me get back to counting."

"I'm very sorry to bother you, sir," said Andy, backing away. "It's just that it's nearly dawn, and I'd hoped—"

"Well, if it will help you leave any faster," interrupted the scorpion, "you might go ask the old cowboy who lives on the hill. I nested in his boot once, on a cold night. Scurry past the big boulder where the moon sets, and you'll find him."
He scuttled away under a stone.

Alone once more, Andy walked on. It was the time of night when all is still. There was no wind and no sound but his own four hooves on the sand.

A little while before dawn Andy found a house. Just outside was a man as old as the hills, playing the banjo.

"Good evening, sir," said Andy. "Or morning, as it may be," he added a bit nervously.

After a long pause the old man spoke. His voice was soft, like hooves on sand, and owl wings, and the movements of dust. "What is it that you want, my friend?" he asked.

"I'm searching for a cake for my friend Cowboy Ned so he can have cake on his birthday," said Andy.

"I have no cake," said the old cowboy. "Out here there would be no one to share it with."

Andy sat down in the dust.

"All I wanted was to give my friend Cowboy Ned a birthday cake so he could have a happy birthday," he said. "But now it's too late."

"Is a cake the only thing that would make Ned happy?" asked the old cowboy.

Andy thought. He thought of a little house out in the desert, and stacks of rocks, and wind, and the campsite far away. "No!" he said. "A cake is very nice to have, but the best thing to have on your birthday is a friend to share it with. I should never have left! A horse doesn't leave his cowboy halfway down the trail."

The old cowboy smiled at Andy.

"Sounds like the best present you can give Ned," he said, "is to be with him on his birthday. Now, go to your friend before dawn."

Andy hurried back, past the scorpion's stone, and the owl on his cactus, and the cricket, who had fallen asleep and was still singing himself a lullaby.

And as he went, he watched the sky, until he saw an edge of it grow pink.

Then, still gazing upward, he began to gallop east, racing the dawn to be with Cowboy Ned on his birthday.

At the campsite he found Cowboy Ned and all the cows waiting for him.

The sun was coming up. It was Ned's birthday.

Cowboy Ned hugged Andy, and Andy wished him a happy birthday.

And all the cows sang a birthday song in their low and
gentle voices.

And somewhere nearby, a banjo joined in.